The Best Laid Plan

Publication Date: September 10, 2018

AQUARIOTS
U N L I M I T E D

ISBN-13: 978-1-7750252-3-8

Chapter 1

Emmilene gazed across the road at him with longing eyes. He was ruggedly handsome, with a muscular physique that showed itself even beneath his layers and overcoat, which were worn with a casual disregard. His light brown, almost ginger hair was thick and upswept at the ends, and his scruffy triangular beard had longer tufts at the corners of his jawline. He didn't have the same concern for decorous grooming as did other gentlemen, which made for a rather untamed, but undeniably attractive, appearance. His name was Roderick Ruttledge, and he was the most affluent bachelor in the city. But money didn't matter to Emmilene. All she wanted was the chance to love him in person.

She'd seen him around town many times before, and each glimpse was a delight. Everyone knew who he was on sight. He often had some young lady or other on his arm — showing her around and taking her to lavish events. Emmilene wished she could be one of those girls, just so she could spend time with him.

Roderick came here to the inn every day at noon, to chat with the newspaper man at his stall before giving him a fivepence tip and going inside for lunch. After noticing Roderick at that spot one time, Emmilene started returning daily to watch him for the ten minutes he spent there. But she stayed on the far side of the street; it would be improper for a woman to approach a man. And without being introduced, at that. Not that her family could have done so for her, since they weren't wealthy or prestigious enough to be socializing with a man of his class. However, if Roderick was the one to choose her, that was another matter. So Emmilene waited, and hoped one day he would look her way.

***

Roderick stood speaking with the newsvendor. After the man finished what he was saying, he looked across the street at a young woman in a pastel-green dress. "You know, that poor girl's been pining after you for the longest time."

Roderick turned his eyes to her with appraising interest. "Really?" He hadn't noticed her before. She *was* quite comely, with a wavy mass of golden-brown hair, and a pleasing figure; still slim, but with all the right curves.

"Comes here every day, same time as you, like clockwork. Just to stare at you with those doe eyes."

If she already fancied herself infatuated with him, that would make it all the easier to get her into bed. Roderick toyed with the idea for a moment, then decided to humour her. He was going to make her day.

***

As Emmilene watched, Roderick

began to cross the street to her. Her breath caught, hope leaping within her. *Can it be?* His gaze was definitely on her. He came right up to her, and it was almost surreal. She'd never been this close to him before.

"I hear you've been admiring me," Roderick purred, slowly lifting her hand to give it a kiss, meeting her eyes all the while. "Let me return the favour."

She stared at him with big eyes, and dipped a brief curtsy. "You are too kind, Mr. Ruttledge," she murmured breathlessly.

He showed a slight smile, eyes glittering. "Call me Roderick," he invited instead. Emmilene's heart was beating fast. "What might your name be?"

"Emmilene. Emmilene Hetherley." Her wish was finally coming to pass! He was actually speaking with her!

"A name well suited to your beauty.

Tell me, Miss Emmilene...have you yet been to see the new clocktower?" He offered his arm.

She could hardly believe he wanted to accompany her somewhere. She tentatively set her hand in the crook of his arm, and couldn't help noticing how muscular it felt, even through the coatsleeve.

They turned to start strolling along together, and Roderick continued to coax comments out of her with leading remarks of his own.

Over an hour later, after they'd toured the outside of the tower, he kissed her hand again and invited her to join him on the morrow at the tea shop. Emmilene could hardly contain her excitement as she agreed. As soon as Roderick had gone on by, she set a hand over her heart in an attempt to calm herself. *He wants to see me again!*

Roderick came to meet her every day, and they spent progressively longer amounts of time together. He flirted and teased and charmed and romanced, making clear his intention to woo her. He escorted her to banquets where they sampled fine cuisine; to ballrooms where they danced hand-in-hand; to plays of a dramatic romantic nature that often made her gasp and set a hand on his arm; and to boutiques where he bought her anything she fancied, no matter how pricy. Emmilene found it all very glamorous, but what she cherished most was just being in his company, all the talk they shared; what she thought and felt, their lives and interests, or just pleasant repartee for the enjoyment of it.

Roderick took every opportunity to get closer to her; helping her down from carriages, guiding her with a hand on her back, letting her use his arm as a brace as she stepped over puddles. Though they'd only known each other for a few weeks, Emmilene didn't mind; she could imagine every touch was an indication of his affection for her. He gave her gifts of jewelry and perfumes, and murmured sweet sentiments in her ear. He made her feel so treasured. She was sure it meant he was starting to care for her as much as she did for him.

One night, he took her to the biggest ball of the season, held in the grand hall, where every local notable personage would be in attendance. Emmilene wore her best new gown of navy blue satin, along with white elbow-length gloves. Roderick held her close as they danced for hours, sweeping across the floor amidst a heady blur of enveloping music and other couples. It seemed at once to last for a dreamlike lifetime and to be over too soon. When she and Roderick finally left and proceeded down the wide stone steps, she was still rosy-cheeked from the activity, rhapsodizing to him about the experience as they walked across the square.

She was in too much of a whirl of exhilaration to realize he'd backed her into a corner. She only broke off from her breathless enthusing when she glanced up to see him watching her with an intense gaze. Before she could react, he slid his gloved hand onto the side of her face, and leaned in to give her an ardent kiss.

Her heart leapt with surprised delight. The feel of his ginger stubble brushing her skin, the feel of his moist lips on hers, touched her so tenderly, so deeply, that she was filled with affectionate adoration for him. Oh, it was just what she'd always wanted!

His other hand was resting on her waist, and she set her own on his arm. Emmilene knew it was scandalous for an unmarried couple to kiss, but at this point she didn't care — and it bespoke of further intentions he must have for their future.

When at last he pulled away, it left her heart racing and her body atingle with warmth. Roderick met her gaze from a few inches away, dark eyes twinkling.

Emmilene glanced down demurely, then lifted her eyes to his again, harbouring a small smile.

It was then that she knew she was in love with him.

From then on, they became even closer, touching more often and stealing occasional kisses where no one would see.

One summer afternoon, they were strolling down the sidewalk with Emmilene's arms wrapped around his. Watching her, Roderick leaned a bit closer. "It's sweltering out here, isn't it," he purred. "It's only a block to my apartment suite. Shall we head inside?"

Emmilene studied him. It was inadvisable for a young woman to be alone with a man in his own residence. But she trusted Roderick. She nodded.

He showed her into his building, and they went up to his rooms on the third floor. He got the door for her, then followed her in. With his hands on the knob behind him, he leaned back on the door to quietly close it, watching her with lowered brows while she drifted in to the middle of the drawing room.

It was a luxurious place, furnished with upholstered seats and varnished tables that still contributed a sense of masculine independence. The russet wallpaper made the room look even warmer than it already was with the summer sunlight coming in.

Roderick crossed to the window, and lowered the sash. He turned back to Emmilene, meeting her eyes with a simmering gaze. The still air was thick with allure. Roderick came slowly over to her, until he stood very close. "Emmilene…I must profess what I feel for you."

Her heartbeat quickened with expectant joy. Could it be that Roderick loved her too?

"Every day I've spent with you has made it grow stronger." He rested his hand on her waist. "I can't keep resisting it. I know you feel it too." Roderick inched his face beside hers, and the proximity made warmth rise in her cheeks. And…elsewhere.

"All your wildest fantasies…" Roderick murmured by her ear, his breath warm on her neck. "All the things you've never felt..." He stroked the backs of his fingers over her shoulder. "All the intimacy you desire..." He drew her hips closer with his other hand, and Emmilene felt a surge of yearning. "I can give it to you."

Her breathing became shaky.

Roderick turned his head, his lips hovering near her cheek. "Will you let me?"

Emmilene shuddered with temptation. "Yes," she breathed.

He stooped and kissed her, more deeply and lingeringly than ever before. The feel of him inside her mouth made her loins kindle with juicy stirrings. His burst of passion was overwhelming, and it left her rather breathless.

His presence was so magnetic, his untucked shirt so enticing, Emmilene couldn't withhold the urge to explore him.

She slid her hands up under his shirt, feeling the firm muscles of his bare torso. Roderick spared her the trouble and pulled his shirt off over his head, tossing it heedlessly to the floor. Then he sank his hands in her mass of hair, holding her face between both of them as he engaged her mouth with his again.

Roderick advanced so she had to step backwards along with him. He backed her up against the wall rather firmly, cornering her there with his sinewy arms on either side of her. Emmilene was quivering all over, but it was from anticipation. The moment she'd long been dreaming of was about to happen! She loved him so much, she gave nary a thought to expressing it before their wedding. She looped her arms onto his shoulders, and laced her fingers behind his neck. Roderick pressed his body against hers, so very warm, and…masculine.

He hoisted her legs up onto his hips, so her draping skirt concealed everything below their waists. With her head now slightly above his, Roderick pinned her against the wall.

As they resumed kissing, Emmilene curled her fingers into the longer tufts of his ginger side-whiskers, clutching them between her knuckles. The tingles he made her body feel were as hot as ginger, too.

Chapter 2

In the days that followed, Emmilene all too aware that Roderick didn't come to visit her. When she received no word from him either, she went to the same place she had first met him. He arrived there on time, as always. He saw her too, she was sure of it; their eyes met briefly across the distance. But he didn't come over to her, didn't even acknowledge her with a wave, nod, or smile – he just went about his business like she wasn't there. Maybe he was just otherwise occupied, and would call on her when he could. Emmilene returned every day to wait for him, just as she had before – but Roderick never crossed to her, even as the days turned into weeks. She didn't understand it. She just hoped that, in time, he would come back to her.

One afternoon, she kept gazing after him even after he had gone inside the inn. At least this way, she got to see him for a little while each day.

A carriage came barrelling up the puddle-ridden street, and she jumped back on the sidewalk to avoid the splash. She bumped into the chest of someone, who set steadying hands on her shoulders. Surprised, Emmilene tilted her head back to look up at the tanned, almost olive-skinned face above her, which belonged to a tall, dark-haired young lieutenant in a drab-green uniform. "Oh." Emmilene chuckled sheepishly, hastily sidestepping out of his way and turning to face him. "Pardon me."

His expression was accommodating, though, and faintly amused. "It's quite all right," he reassured. Then his face became curious. "What's a young lady like yourself doing waiting out here on a corner? I've seen you at this same spot a few times."

Emmilene lowered her eyes, then looked out across the street again. "I just come here to get a glimpse of the man who used to court me."

The lieutenant's brow furrowed. "He

doesn't call on you anymore?"

"We haven't met in weeks." She sighed. "I'm sure Roderick will find the time soon."

"Roderick?" the lieutenant repeated. "That wouldn't perchance be Roderick Ruttledge? I know him!"

She turned to the man in delight. "You do?"

"He and I have been friends since we were boys. I'm Ishwar Langhorne."

She offered her hand in introduction. "Emmilene Hetherley."

He paused in taking her hand. "You're *that* Emmilene?" he remarked. "He's told me all about you."

Her heart lifted. "He speaks of me? Will you talk with me about him?"

Ishwar's expression sobered a little, and he gestured toward the sidewalk. "Shall we go for a stroll?" Emmilene took the arm he offered, and they turned to start walking.

They talked about Roderick for hours, Ishwar sharing stories of their childhood. Emmilene and the lieutenant met again over the next few days, and they soon became well acquainted.

When they came to a teahouse, Ishwar sat down with her on a bench outside it. The lieutenant's face was earnest. "I know you only want to hear the best of Roderick, but you must know why he hasn't been seeing you anymore." He waited, but she didn't respond. "That man is a rake, Emmilene," he imparted to her, solemn and regretful. "He doesn't care for you, and he never did. All you ever were to him was a pretty skirt to chase."

She was silent for a moment. "You don't speak of him as a friend," she observed instead.

Ishwar showed a wry smile. "I've known for years what kind of man he is; it takes a certain lenience to be his friend anyway. I'm saying it outright so that you too will understand his nature for what it is."

"I already knew he was partial to dalliance," Emmilene said quietly. "But what we had was more than that. I know he'll come to see that, too."

"I admire your loyalty," Ishwar remarked, with genuine surprise. "But I doubt it'll make any difference to him. He's done this before; charmed a lady until he got what he wanted from her, then left her in the lurch." He lowered his voice, watching her gently. "He boasted to me of his conquest of you. I know the two of you were intimate together."

Her cheeks grew hot to hear it spoken of by another — but just as much of it was from remembering the pleasure of her time with Roderick. "I have no regrets."

"I think you need to fully consider what he's done to you. Once they find out you've already been with a man, no one will want to marry you."

Emmilene looked up with some concern. But she was more resigned than devastated.

"No one, that is, except me. I'd be willing to overlook that and be a husband to you anyway. I could provide you with a secure future, and a respectable standing."

She almost considered that for a moment. Then she dropped her eyes. "That's very kind of you," she murmured. "But it won't be necessary."

Ishwar inclined his head. "Very well," he replied. "But I suggest that you at least stop waiting for him every day. If it hasn't garnered his attention after two weeks, it's not going to. Your time would be better spent starting to move on."

Emmilene looked down the street, toward the inn. "I will always wait for him."

And so she did. But every time, after Roderick just went on his way again, Ishwar came around to keep her company. He even insisted on taking her to events so she wouldn't miss out, and also brought her to meet his parents and his sister Indira, who took to Emmilene like a sister herself.

***

Roderick saw Emmilene across the road several times without giving her a second thought. But after a while, he found himself thinking of her on occasion, even while going about his day. It was just a snippet here and there; a memory of her inviting green eyes, the floral scent of her perfume, the way her warm, soft body felt on his. And once it came to him, he ended up dwelling on it longer. No other girl had lingered in his mind so. He began to feel something – a yearning – that could even be called nostalgia. He wanted to have her again. Maybe he shouldn't have been so hasty to leave her. Perhaps, with her especial willingness, he could have gotten a few more times out of her before she began expecting a commitment. Maybe he still could, if she was patient enough to be waiting for him every day.

Roderick walked up the street one day, and spotted Emmilene on the other side. She hadn't noticed him yet. He regarded her for a moment, pausing, then decided to go up to her. He crossed the road, weaving between the other people pushing handcarts or leading donkeys. Then he started up the sidewalk toward her, passing by a window display of a dress shop. As he neared where the jutting building formed a nook, he slowed, stopping to look at Emmilene past the corner. She was still gazing across at the inn he usually frequented.

But he found himself faced with a most unfamiliar hesitation. He'd never gone back to a girl after he'd had his way with her. And Roderick Ruttledge wasn't the one to supplicate women. They were the ones who lined up for a chance to be with him. What was he to even say to explain his absence? It had been weeks already; Emmilene probably didn't want anything to do with him anymore. He would just be setting himself up for rejection. If it had been anyone else, it wouldn't have mattered to him.

Then a young woman joined

Emmilene, who turned to her to give her a hug of glad welcome.

Roderick's heart sank a little in resignation. He'd missed his chance. He couldn't speak with her now, when she had company. Besides, it looked like she was moving on with her life; just there to meet a friend, not gaze across the road at him anymore.

Slowly, he backed away from the corner, then turned and walked away.

Chapter 3

Roderick sat sprawled in a chair with one arm on his desk, his back to the large windows of his apartment study. He stared at the glass of gin in his hand, then downed another swallow of it. He felt numb inside, and not just from the liquor.

Emmilene was still on his mind. Why hadn't he gone up to her? He'd never lost his gumption like that before. He had always been the master of confidence.

The door opened, and Ishwar strolled in without knocking. He was all neat and proper in his olive-drab uniform, in contrast to Roderick's untucked shirt and unbuttoned coat.

Roderick eyed him expressionlessly. He wasn't in the mood for company right now.

"You look miserable," Ishwar remarked cheerfully. "Care to air your woes to a sympathetic ear?"

Roderick swirled the gin in his glass. "Not – in – the slightest," he articulated crisply. He took another drink.

"Well, then, I'll just carry on with

what I came here to say," Ishwar went on briskly, and pulled up a chair. "Remember your latest conquest, Emmilene?"

Roderick glanced up, attention piqued at the echo of his thoughts.

"I've met her; she's quite a lovely thing. She and I are courting now, as it happens."

Roderick watched him flatly. Was Ishwar trying to make him jealous? It wouldn't work; Roderick never got emotionally attached to any of his flings. After he was done with them, he couldn't care less who got involved with them next.

"We've laid together, quite a few times." Ishwar grew a smirk. "You're right, she is quite the passionflower in bed."

Roderick's gaze hardened. He was beginning to feel a stir of resentment in spite of himself. To hear the lieutenant talk about

Emmilene that way, so insolently…to imagine Ishwar defiling her, the same woman Roderick had been with first…it *did* make him seethe. No one had ever flaunted their appropriation of his erstwhile lover.

"But even when we're making love, all she can talk about is you. She kept comparing it to her time with you, and she says you were better." Ishwar paused to study him. "She must still be deeply in love with you. Even after I told her all about your previous exploits, she didn't change her mind about you. That's some kind of dedication." His expression became stern. "It was wrong of you to toy with her affections," he chided. "A good woman like her doesn't deserve that."

Roderick felt a twinge, and dropped his eyes. He felt bad about hurting her. Was this…guilt?

"And based on your most

uncharacteristic melancholy, I'd say you care for her just as much."

Roderick flicked his eyes up to Ishwar in surprise.

"Consider it, now. Can you honestly say you don't?"

Roderick's absent gaze drifted aside. Whenever he thought of Emmilene, he envisioned her waves of golden-brown hair, her radiant smile...the spark they'd had together. He wanted that again. And without her now, he felt empty. He'd never experienced these emotions for anyone else before. Could it be love?

Roderick sighed. "What do you suggest I do?"

"Marry her," Ishwar stated simply, and Roderick glanced up at him. "I know such a thought has never crossed your mind before, but you won't find another woman as devoted as she is. It's the decent thing to do, and you're the only one she'll be happy with. If you care about her at all, you'll want that for her."

And Ishwar left him to contemplate that. Roderick tried to find if there was any reason he shouldn't marry her. Her family was much less wealthy than his. But he had no need to marry for money. There certainly wasn't anyone else he could think of that he'd rather spend a lifetime with. He shuddered at the thought. Most of the other girls he'd dallied with were insufferably featherbrained, or had irritating mannerisms, or weren't all that pretty to begin with. He hadn't even liked them. He'd only been in it for the conquest, whether or not they were pleasant company.

Emmilene, though...she was refined, yet wholesome; intelligent, but gentle. There wasn't a single thing about her that was disagreeable. Roderick could imagine her making the ideal wife; docile and patient and willing. And then he wouldn't have to look further than his own wife for gratification.

Of course, then he couldn't enjoy the thrill of pursuing new women, either. But at a certain point, the turnaround time between scores became tiresome anyway. And much as he hated to admit it, there might eventually come a time — many decades from now — when he might not be able to attract the eyes of young ladies quite the same. If he married now, he wouldn't have to worry about that, even if that meant not taking advantage of all those perfectly good years of eligibility. Besides, there was no guarantee that anyone he found from now on would be any better a catch than Emmilene.

The next evening, Roderick walked to

the Hetherley townhouse on the southeast side of town. He went up the stone steps, and paused before using the brass doorknocker. He wasn't used to taking the polite approach, but he was in a position of supplication this time, so it wouldn't do to barge in uninvited.

The door was opened by the doorman, and Roderick told him he'd come to see Emmilene. The man let Roderick in and closed the door behind him.

"Mr. Ruttledge has come calling," the doorman announced, then withdrew into another room.

Emmilene drifted into the foyer, and hopeful warmth lit in her eyes when she saw him. "Roderick," she murmured.

Her reception was encouraging. He stepped a bit closer. "I know it's been too long. But I'm here now. You've been on my mind ever since, like no one else ever has.

What I mean to say is..." He took her hands in his. "I...I've come to have a deep and indelible love for you."

Her breath caught. "Oh, Roderick!" she breathed, and wrapped her arms about his neck in a hug.

He drew Emmilene close to him, his heart filling with a most affectionate and poignant sensation, stronger than even he would have expected. It felt so good to hold her. Her body fit so perfectly against his own. Her sweet nature, that he was now so fond of, emanated from every soft, warm contour of her figure.

Roderick backed up a little to meet her eyes. "There's something I must ask you," he went on. "I don't even know how to pose it, for I've never asked it before, nor even considered it." He lifted her hand in both of his. "Will you be my wife?"

Eyes big and glistening, Emmilene set her fingertips to her mouth for a moment, partially covering a quivering smile. "I've been waiting months to say yes to that," she whispered.

Breaking into a lopsided grin, Roderick set his hands on either side of her face and leaned in to kiss her. Her moist, full lips were just as luscious as he remembered, the spark they kindled within him just as strong. Emmilene set her hands on his chest, and willingly reciprocated. His desire simmered to life again, spurred by how attracted he was to her. He lingered on her round lower lip, then gave her another kiss. He didn't want to stop kissing her, but he reluctantly restrained himself; this was neither the time nor the place for what he wanted to do. He stayed with his forehead bowed against hers, their warm breaths a bit unsteady on each other's faces.

"Shall we sit?" Emmilene suggested. She pulled back, and they adjourned into the parlour, settling onto a settee. She leaned closer to him, resting her shoulder on his chest.

"I suppose you know you're not the only woman I've laid with." Roderick fixed his stony gaze on the floor. "I don't blame you for doing the same with Ishwar."

Emmilene drew back abruptly, looking at him with a scandalized frown. "What? I never sought those comforts from him. We only ever conversed as friends."

He stared at her. Then he realized. Ishwar must have just told him that to get him riled up. Roderick was on the verge of becoming indignant, but then had to admit that it had worked. It was a good thing, too; it was what it had taken to get him to go back to her. He studied Emmilene with wondering admiration. "Your loyalty is unequalled." He'd done nothing to earn it.

Her eyes drifted shyly down to his hand where it rested on his knee, and she entwined her fingers with his. "You're the only one I've ever wanted," she said softly. She set her head on his shoulder. "Now we can give our families the good news."

Roderick wasn't looking forward to that. His parents were sure to frown upon it, since they would consider Emmilene beneath his station. But he supposed it had to be done. They'd done enough sneaking around. She deserved to at least have her wedding be a public occasion.

Chapter 4

On the morrow, Roderick went to the Ruttledge estate, situated some distance outside the south end of town. A long, winding gravel laneway ended in a circle before the front steps. It was an impressive mansion of sandstone and dark grey slate roofs, with plenty of rock garden landscaping.

Roderick informed his parents that he intended to host a dinner at the manor. Then he had invitation notes delivered to Emmilene's family, and to the Langhornes as well, to show Ishwar that Roderick had taken his advice to heart.

After dark, the Hetherleys arrived first in a carriage, followed by Ishwar and his parents. As they disembarked, Roderick went out to accompany Emmilene, and the butler saw the rest of them in.

They all met in the dining hall. Roderick and Emmilene sat beside each other, while her parents were given the seats of honour at the head of the long table. Everyone exchanged the usual pleasantries, but none of them appeared as if they knew what they were gathered for – all looking from one to the other for clues. Mrs. Ruttledge, with her blonde hair up in a tight bun that accentuated her sharp features, was eyeing the plump and almost folksy Mrs. Hetherley with disdain. Red-haired Mr. Ruttledge idly ran the back of a thumbnail over one of his mutton-chop sideburns as he regarded Mr. Langhorne. After the glasses of wine had been served, but before the food arrived, Roderick spoke up.

"The reason I've invited you all here is to make an announcement." Roderick studied each of their faces. "Emmilene and I are engaged to be married."

There was a floored silence.

"Married? To *her*?" Mrs. Ruttledge repeated. "Why, she's little more than a commoner."

"Come now, Roderick," Mr. Ruttledge scoffed. "We all know you're not the type to settle down."

Roderick compressed his lips with flat determination. "I assure you, I have every intention of marrying her."

Mrs. Hetherley had her hand to her mouth, looking from Ishwar to Emmilene and back. "Oh, dear, this is a dreadful mistake," she murmured.

Roderick bristled. "Make no mistake, this is just as much Emmilene's decision as it is mine."

"You don't understand — this arrangement is simply not possible," Mr. Langhorne put in. "For the simple fact that she is already betrothed to our son."

Roderick stared at the man, speechless. Then he looked at Ishwar. The lieutenant wore a rather smug look. *What...?* Then Roderick set his jaw, and stood up so his chair scraped back over the floor. "I don't know what you're playing at, but this farce changes nothing," he growled. He took Emmilene's hand, and she rose, too. "Emmilene and I will be wed, with or without your approval."

With that, he turned and stormed out with her. After a pause, the room behind him erupted into commotion. From the sound of it, they were just getting in each other's way.

Then footsteps followed them, and Roderick looked over his shoulder to see Ishwar sauntering out from the archway.

"Wait outside," he muttered to Emmilene without looking back at her. After she was out the door, Roderick advanced on Ishwar.

"What is the meaning of this?" he demanded. "I thought you told me to marry her!"

"Indeed I did," Ishwar admitted

calmly, with a trace of a smirk. "But I didn't say I'd make it easy for you."

Roderick stared at him for a consternated moment. "How do you know I won't just give her up?"

"Because I know you," he replied simply, but grimly. "You want what you can't have, and you'd never back down from a competition."

Roderick narrowed his eyes. "And I never lose one, either."

Before anyone else could come after them, he spun and strode outside, where Emmilene stood on the porch. Without slowing, he gripped her hand, his fingers linked with hers. As they swiftly descended the stone steps, he looked over at her. "Did you know about this?" It came out a little harsher than he'd intended; he was still fuming at Ishwar.

"No," she murmured sadly, eyes downcast. "I never accepted any proposal. Our parents must have arranged it when they saw that we were spending time together."

She was such a gentle soul. She still thought the best of those who were plotting against them.

They climbed into the waiting carriage, and at Roderick's signal, the driver slapped the reins to set them racing off for the city.

Behind them, Emmilene's parents came rushing out onto the porch and stopped short. "Come back here with our daughter!" Mr. Hetherley called after them. "You have no claim on her!"

Once the Ruttledge house was out of sight, Roderick faced forward again. But his gaze was downturned in frowning thought.

"I can't take you back to your parents'

residence," he said, and Emmilene looked up. "They'd just keep you there, to keep us apart, and force you to marry Ishwar."

Her eyes held concern. "Should we stay at your suite?" she suggested in a small voice.

Roderick met her eyes, tempted by the thought of repeating what they had done the last time they were there. But then he dropped his gaze. "No. That's the first place they'd look," he muttered. He started thinking again, then came up with an alternative. "I'll put you up at a first-rate boardinghouse. Then we'll pick out a bridal dress for you tomorrow. That'll show them we're in earnest."

Roderick leaned over Emmilene's seat and slid the panel open to tell the driver to take them to the new destination on the northwest side of town.

When they got there, Roderick paid for a room on the third floor. He went up with Emmilene and opened the door for her, then followed her in and closed it behind him.

He went to the window, and parted the curtain to peer out at the dark street below, looking up and down it. No one seemed to have followed them there.

He turned back to the room. Emmilene had seated herself on the foot of the bed, and was watching him with upturned eyes. She looked so demure and feminine, with her hands folded in her lap. Roderick became aware of what she must be thinking, with the intimate setting, the quiet depths of the night, just the two of them alone together, finally. He could so easily push her down on the bed...

With an effort, he reined in his desires. "I'll go have the kitchen prepare something for us." They'd left the manor before supper had been served, after all. It was more important that Emmilene not miss a meal.

Roderick went down and brought back a platter of bread and stew-filled bowls himself, so there would be all the less people to see Emmilene and potentially disclose her location. After handing her the tray, he ate his share in a chair by the window as he kept watch.

By the time he was done, Emmilene was sound asleep on the bed, her arms curled up before her. Roderick couldn't help a slight smile of wry fondness. There would be no fooling around tonight. It was only fun if they were awake, anyway. But a touch of tenderness also rose in him. He got up to take a knitted throw from one of the chaises, and settled it over Emmilene. Then he returned to his post to look out into the night.

When morning came, Roderick took her to the dress shop to pick out a wedding gown. Entering the sunny store, they started browsing the racks and wicker figures displaying dresses of both white and all colours.

"Buy whichever dress your heart desires," Roderick told her softly. "Money is no object."

Emmilene looked them over, setting a hand on one to feel the fabric or taking another off the rack to see it full-length.

Behind them, the shop door banged open. "Ruttledge!" a stern voice barked. Roderick turned to see Mr. Langhorne, Ishwar, and Emmilene's father starting toward them, weaving between the dress racks.

Roderick spun and towed Emmilene along by the hand as they dashed for the back door.

The men chased after them, and Roderick dodged out of sight down a side street. But then he spotted Ishwar at the alley mouth trying to head them off, so Roderick had to pull Emmilene into another shop to run out through a side door.

Over the next few hours, there were several more near-misses as the others pursued them through town, but Roderick and Emmilene managed to elude them. After things finally quieted down, Roderick arranged for a carriage to meet them on an empty street. He helped Emmilene into it and closed the door for her.

"Going somewhere?"

Roderick turned to see Ishwar strolling up the street toward them.

"Absconding with a young woman? You should know better."

Roderick took a few strides toward him. "Give up this charade! She never agreed to marry you."

"Either way, she belongs at home until the wedding."

Hooves clattered on cobblestones behind Roderick, and he whirled as the carriage charged away. Emmilene leaned out the window, looking back at him with sorrow in her eyes.

"That'll be her parents now," Ishwar mused.

Roderick glared at him, but the lieutenant was already ducking down a side alley. Ishwar must have planned the whole thing. He always seemed to be one step ahead. Roderick watched the distant carriage, and beat a fist on his thigh, cursing himself for letting it happen. There'd be no point going to the Hetherley townhouse; in all likelihood, they wouldn't even let him in to see her. He was going to have to think of some other way to settle this once and for all.

Chapter 5

Roderick entered the bank to make a withdrawal, but to his disbelief the banker refused his transaction request. When Roderick insisted on knowing why, he was told he no longer had authority to access the account. Roderick turned on his heel and left, heading to the Ruttledge estate to see what this was all about.

On his way through town to find a cheap cabriolet, he noticed people looking at him and shaking their heads in disapproval, muttering amongst themselves. He caught a few snatches of "cad" and "disgrace". He began to feel a creeping apprehension. What rumour was going around about him now?

When he got to the manor, the butler opened the door only a little, and seemed reluctant when Roderick told him to inform the Ruttledges of his arrival. But Roderick pushed past him when he saw his parents in the dim foyer beyond.

"The bank has locked me out. Would you know anything about that?" Roderick demanded of them.

Mr. Ruttledge had his brows drawn

down. "It was our doing. We know all about your many *indiscretions* with women," he hissed.

Roderick stopped short, aghast. How had they found out...?

Mrs. Ruttledge shook her head slowly. "How could you, Roderick?" she whispered.

Mr. Ruttledge's face was stern. "You are a disgrace to this family's name. You are hereby disentitled from all access to our estate."

Roderick stared at him, dread sinking into the pit of his stomach. Then it gave rise to indignation. "You can't disown me! I'm your only heir!"

"We *have* no heir."

Roderick clenched his jaw, then jabbed a finger at them, eyes narrowed. "Don't pretend you didn't know about it all along. You just turned a blind eye to spare your own reputation."

Mr. Ruttledge jerked a nod at the butler, who took Roderick's arm to escort him off the premises, but Roderick yanked free.

"*Don't* have my own butler cast me out!" he snarled. He whirled and stormed out the door, slamming it closed behind him.

Roderick fumed as he strode down the laneway. What was he going to do now? He had no money but the change in his pocket, no possessions but the clothes on his back. He wouldn't be able to replenish his funds, or reside on the estate, or enjoy the free benefits of a high renown. If he didn't find a source of income soon, he wouldn't be able to afford his apartment suite, let alone food. His life as it had been was at an end. But what stung more than being cut off from his family's resources was that his parents had been the ones to forsake him. He would've liked to think they'd be more supportive than that. Now that they'd gone through with it, though, there would be no convincing them to change their minds. He was on his own.

Then his thoughts went to Emmilene. How was he to marry her, when he could bring nothing to the table? He couldn't even buy her a proper wedding dress now!

Roderick returned to his apartment building, but was hardly surprised to find that he'd already been evicted, without even the chance to go up and gather any of his belongings, much less have any furniture relocated.

He slowly turned away and wandered through town.

He didn't even know how to go about getting a job. He tried stopping by the respectable establishments he used to frequent — the haberdashery, the bank, the law office — to see if they were hiring. But, of course, since he had no prior employment experience, none of them wanted him. Some recognized him as the recently disgraced libertine, and turned him down on that basis alone.

As the day grew late and he still had no luck, he realized he'd have to secure a place to stay before nightfall, or he'd be stuck on the streets. So he pawned his silver cufflinks, and used the money to pay half the first month's rent for a room at the cheapest apartment building he could find, which was all it would cover.

Roderick sat on the lumpy cot and looked around at the dingy room. He doubted he could even get to sleep in such a place. His spirit sank along with the deepening gloom.

Over the next few days, he went

hunting for jobs again, inquiring at progressively less dignified places of business until he'd exhausted all but his most desperate options. He returned to his apartment and sat in a rickety chair beside the desk, slumping in it glumly. How he wished he could afford a glass of gin right now.

Footsteps sounded in the hall outside the open door. Roderick lifted his head as Ishwar came by the doorway.

"Ah, how the wealthy have fallen," the lieutenant remarked grandly, striding ponderously into the room. "I thought it was about time your family knew the true nature of your character."

Roderick stared at him. *He* was the one who had done it? "Why?" he breathed. "Why are you doing this? I thought we were friends."

"We were. Until you dallied with my

sister."

Roderick's eyes widened slightly in dismay.

Ishwar cocked his head. "Did you think she wouldn't tell me?"

"Then why all this? Why not just force me to marry your sister?"

"Oh, I want better for Indira than a man like you. You'd just philander with other women behind her back. I needed to teach you a lesson." Slowly, he grew a smile that was almost fervid in its vindictive anticipation. "I'll make an honest man out of you yet."

Roderick was dazed. His life had been single-handedly ruined — by none other than his own lifelong friend, no less — but he'd brought it on himself. And all for what, a shameless dalliance he could just as well have avoided? He had no pride left. He had no money, no good name, no woman, and no prospect of getting any of it back.

Ishwar turned aside, flicking his leather gloves onto his palm. "So you're aware, Emmilene and I will be wed on the twenty-fifth of December." It was like the final blow to Roderick's heart. "However, there is one alternative — if, by that date, you can manage to earn two hundred pounds to buy the marriage license from me, and you bring that sum to the chapel by nine o'clock that morning, you can have Emmilene's hand in marriage." Then he went back out the door.

Roderick felt a ray of hope. There was a chance for him after all. If he had Emmilene, at least, maybe that would be enough to make his new circumstances bearable.

And then he had a realization. Marrying her would mean getting a dowry.

And it would be substantial compared to what he had now. The only way he could have a secure monetary future was if he married into a wealthy family — and that's what Emmilene's was. He'd considered them second-class before, but they were still considerably richer than he could ever hope to become by working a common job, even if he did it for the rest of his life. But first he had to earn enough for the license. Two hundred pounds — an amount he would've easily spent in a week in his old lifestyle. How hard could it be to make that much?

Roderick set out the next day, determined not to come back until he had acquired a job. He searched high and low for hours, until finally he found an opening at a place that would take him, at the sawpits in the southwest half of town, cutting boards for use in construction.

He started work there first thing the following morning, and was shown the ropes. Then he was assigned to the lower role down in the stone-walled pit, to cut long logs into planks with a two-man saw, while the more experienced top sawyer made sure to guide the blade straight. Even after the two of them finally established some semblance of coordination, it was still grueling work — messy too, with sawdust constantly sifting down around Roderick. It seemed to go on forever, with hardly a five-minute break every hour. Despite the October air, the sun beating down on him in the pit made him swelter just as much as the exertion.

When he came back to his apartment at the end of the day, he was covered in grime and smelled of sawdust. All his muscles ached; he'd never worked them so long or hard in his life. All he wanted to do was take a long hot bath — but even that was a luxury now, one that he couldn't afford more than once a week. He had to settle for a spongedown with a bucket of water heated in the fireplace.

Roderick was still sore the next morning, but he reported for duty again, and persevered for the rest of the week.

When he received his first salary, he was appalled at how meagre it was. All that work, and this is what he got for it? It was barely enough to buy a decent pair of boots! He used it to pay for his room and board, but there was hardly anything left after that. As the weeks went on, he calculated how much he'd earn over the next two months and how much of it he'd have to spend on essentials, and realized he wouldn't be able to save enough at this rate. He started cutting corners, no longer purchasing clothes to restock his wardrobe, and buying less food for himself — but that wasn't going to make enough of a difference, either. He'd never had to budget his expenditures this carefully before. He began working longer hours, even taking over shifts from the other workers.

Roderick was passing by his window one day when he glimpsed a familiar figure on the street below. A weight lifted from his chest. "Emmilene," he murmured. Cloaked in a satin hood, she darted across the road to his building and looked both ways down the sidewalk, then entered.

Roderick raced down several flights of stairs, and came to the dim foyer to find Emmilene pushing her hood back as she cast around. When their eyes met, glad yearning came over her face.

She hastened over to him and took his hands. "My family won't let me come and see you anymore, now that they know your reputation. I just barely managed to slip away."

Roderick was tired of playing by Ishwar's rules. His gaze became earnest. "Let's leave town together. Get married on our own terms."

Emmilene stared at him in wonder. Then her eyes saddened. "We can't run," she murmured. "You have no money. What will we live on?"

He lowered his eyes, dissatisfied, but resigned. "You're right. We have to do this the proper way." Then he met her gaze again with renewed determination, and held her face in his hands. "But I promise I'll get you back. I *will*." He looked into her eyes for another moment, then brought her over and kissed her. As always, once was never enough, and they soon became carried away. Roderick sank his fingers in her hair, and she looped her arms atop his shoulders, pressing herself against him. A familiar fire started up in him. He stroked a hand up the side of her slim waist, daringly close to her bosom.

Emmilene gave a faint moan, and set her hand on the side of his face, then pulled back from the kiss. "I can't stay long," she murmured with regret, eyes still closed. "They'll wonder where I am."

Pressing his lips together as he resisted the urge to kiss her again, Roderick leaned against her with his forehead, and drew her body snug to his with one hand. It would be so easy to take her up to his room so they could finish what they'd started... He wanted her so bad. "Just two more months," he reassured, and gave her one last ardent kiss.

Then Emmilene was turning away, and their hands stayed linked for another moment before she was out the door.

***

Emmilene stood gazing out the drawing room window, hugging her arms. It wasn't much of a view, from the upper floor at the back of her parents' townhouse. But her mind was elsewhere. She reminisced on her recent rendezvous with Roderick; how he'd smelled of sawdust, in a way that was still somehow enticingly masculine...how he'd felt even more muscular than before.

Boots clicked on the floorboards behind her as Ishwar came in. She turned to him, face troubled. "Why won't you call this off?" she pleaded. "I want to marry Roderick, and he wants to marry me."

The lieutenant's expression was sympathetic. "I know you didn't ask for this.

And I don't wish to cause you distress. But you must be patient. Either he'll get his act together in time, and you'll live blithely forever after — or he won't, and he never deserved to have you anyway. At least then, you'll still have a decent marriage to support you."

"But he *would* have married me, if he hadn't been stripped of his funds."

"That would've been too easy. He needed to be taken down a notch. 'In poverty and in wealth', after all. Even if he married you as easily as he's always gotten everything, there's no guarantee he'd stay faithful to you when times got tough. I'm merely grooming him to be a good husband to you." Ishwar showed a bit of a teasing smirk. "You'll thank me later." Then he turned and walked back out of the room.

Chapter 6

The partner Roderick was paired with at the sawpit was a lanky fellow with unkempt mousy hair and a wide mouth. Roderick didn't even catch his name the first few times, but he was quite the talkative one, often trying to engage Roderick in conversation or otherwise blithely chattering on for hours about everything under the sun, even over the sound of the rasping wood. Roderick for the most part tuned it out, rarely making – or needing to make – a response. He concentrated on thoughts of Emmilene, maintaining his determination to earn her back, just to get through the day's work.

But after a while, some of the details about the fellow's life began to sink in, and Roderick came to know him as Norrill Wexley. They began to share some dialogue, and gradually became friends. When he asked Roderick why he was so preoccupied, he told Wexley about Emmilene and how he'd have to earn enough to get her back. Wexley was enrapt and sympathetic, and wanted to do whatever he could to help, even recommending a part-time task that Roderick could do on the side for some extra money: unloading a cartful of barrels into a tavern every dawn and midnight. It didn't pay much, but neither did other odd jobs, and Roderick didn't have time for anything more than that. At least he got his wages on the spot, and he needed every bit he could get.

He kept it up through to the end of November, and his savings steadily grew, until he had over a hundred pounds.

The beginning of the month came around again, and so did his landlord, to collect his rent. Roderick pled with the man to grant him an extension, just until the end of December — since, if he paid it now, there was no way he'd have enough for the marriage license. After much reluctance, the landlord finally agreed, but only on the condition that Roderick would pay both months' rent first thing in the new year.

Then there was only a week left until the wedding, and Roderick feared he'd still be short by too much. Wexley offered him all twenty pounds of his own savings, meagre as they were. Roderick was astounded that a man with a wife and young children to provide for would give every spare penny he had to someone he'd only met a few months ago. It appeared some commoners were noble after all. Roderick assured him he'd pay it back as soon as he could; either the contribution would make his total amount to enough, and he'd marry Emmilene, whereupon her dowry would certainly cover the loan — or, if he still couldn't scrounge up the full two hundred pounds, he wouldn't be needing to use all of it anymore anyway.

Roderick started skipping meals, so as to spend that much less. Wexley was kind enough to share some of his work lunches with him, and even invited him to supper at his house, as often as Roderick could make it. The days almost blurred into each other; Roderick worked sixteen-hour double shifts, topped by his cask hauls, all the way up until the 24th.

It was late into the night when he finally got back to his apartments. He dropped his coin pouch onto the desk with a sigh. His last pay before the fateful day. It better be enough. He plunked himself down into the chair, and dumped out all his savings onto the table, to start slowly counting it up.

He'd hardly eaten — and slept even less — for days, and his mind was so drowsy and muddled it was hard to keep track of what he was doing, or if he was even doing it correctly, just from one moment to the next. Sometimes he stacked several banknotes without paying attention, and other times he was sure he'd assigned the wrong value to one of them, which made him backtrack to check, but that often confused matters further. He kept nodding off where he sat, only to jerk awake a second later, having forgotten what number he'd just gotten up to — so he had to start all over again. He never got very far. More than once, he did doze off entirely, often dreaming that he was still counting, so when he woke, he was certain he remembered the right amount — but that was impossible, since it was much too high; into the sixteen hundreds. He had no idea how long his naps lasted, but he went back to the task at hand with twice as much urgency to make up for it. Before he knew it, dawn was lightening the overcast sky out the window, and he still hadn't finished tallying it up. At least, he didn't think he had.

There was a brisk knocking on the

door, and then Wexley came right in without waiting for an answer. "It's quarter to nine!" he announced, then stopped short when he saw Roderick. "Why aren't you ready?"

"I'm counting," he mumbled without looking up. He paused. "Where was I?" His sluggish brain churned on that for a moment. "One hundred and ninety pounds and...eighteen pence?" Or was it eighty? No, it must have been eighteen. He went back to it, meticulously adding crowns together to make a pound, then shillings, then going penny by penny.

Wexley went to stand by the foot of the cot behind him and waited. Time dragged on.

"...thirty-eight, thirty-nine...forty." Roderick stared dully at the last penny. A hundred and ninety-nine pounds and forty pence. Could he really be short by only sixty pence? He groaned. If he had come that close, only to fail, he'd surely lose his sanity.

His soul was filled with anguished yearning. *Emmilene...!*

Arms sprawled over the tabletop, Roderick bowed his head and rested it on the wood. After a minute he muttered tonelessly to his friend, "Will you tell them that they've either broken my heart, or broken my mind?"

"Tell them yourself!" Wexley rallied, coming over to roust him out of the chair. "You've come too far to give up now. The wedding's in ten minutes! Just grab all you've got and let's hope it's enough!"

Roderick scooped all his hard-earned money into a sack, and then Wexley hustled him out the door. Roderick was still so tired, his friend had to guide him by the forearm to make sure he didn't stumble or bump into anything. They descended the staircases to the ground floor as swiftly as they could, and the rush of the moment made Roderick more alert. They hurried out onto the street to hail down a hansom cab; Wexley told the driver to make all due haste to the chapel, and they bucketed through town at a reckless gallop.

The cab pulled up in front of the flight of stone steps just as Emmilene and Ishwar were reaching the top, where the priest waited at his podium.

"Wait!" Roderick called, holding up the pouch as he ran up the stairs, trailed by Wexley. "Stay the ceremony!"

Emmilene turned, and her face bloomed into a smile of joyous relief to see that he had come. Ishwar wore a certain complacent look too.

Roderick arrived in front of the priest, panting, and offered the bag. "I've come to buy the marriage license from

Ishwar."

"Is this two hundred pounds?" the priest prompted as he took the pouch.

"I'm…not sure," Roderick admitted.

The priest poured the coins and banknotes out onto the podium before him, then started briskly adding it all up.

Roderick met Emmilene's eyes, which were as anxious and filled with yearning as his own must be. She looked so beautiful in her lacy wedding dress.

The priest began counting aloud as he neared the end. "One ninety-nine thirty…"

Roderick's heart pounded, and he hardly breathed as he anticipated the dreaded shortfall. How would he bear the expression on Emmilene's face when she realized he'd failed her…?

"…forty…fifty…"

Roderick looked at the priest in

surprise as he surpassed his own estimate. Then hope rose in his chest. Roderick himself must have miscounted. Maybe he really did have more than he thought!

"…ninety-eight…ninety-nine…two hundred pounds."

Triumph soared within Roderick. It was just enough!

The priest gathered all the money up into the bag again, then handed Roderick the marriage license. "It's yours to sign."

Roderick looked to Emmilene in wonder. Ishwar, smiling, graciously stepped aside to let Roderick come and stand by Emmilene instead.

She took Roderick's hand, gazing into his eyes. "Oh, Roderick," she breathed. "I knew you could do it."

He squeezed her hand — victorious, but still too exhausted to speak.

The priest opened the doors to lead the way into the dim chapel, and Roderick and Emmilene followed down the aisle together, with Ishwar bringing up the rear. The priest spread his hands as he passed between the guests seated on the pews. "There's been a slight change of plans," he declared. "The groom today will be Roderick Ruttledge."

There were several gasps and mutters, accompanied by creaking as people twisted around in their seats to look back at them.

The priest proceeded to the altar, and Roderick and Emmilene came to stand side-by-side facing him, while Ishwar took a seat on a front bench beside his parents.

The ceremony began with the usual speech, but Roderick barely heard. He was busy taking in the sight of Emmilene's face, imagining what it would be like once she was his wife. He didn't even care that he must look like a dishevelled beggar – and Emmilene didn't seem to mind either. He'd been waiting for this so long, he just wanted it to be official already.

Then it was time for the signing. The priest's assistant came over with a fountain pen and a small table that he set before them for Roderick to place the license on. As the priest spoke the words that they each replied to with "I do", Roderick signed on the lower left, then handed the pen to Emmilene, who wrote her name in an elegant script on the right. They turned to each other. Almost before the priest finished saying they were married, Roderick took Emmilene's face in his hands and kissed her, so passionately that there were some murmurs of surprised disapproval from the more decorous guests. So what if it wasn't part of the ceremony. She was his wife now. Several moments later, Roderick parted from a rather breathless Emmilene. She bit her lip, eyeing him with a coy smile. His gaze smouldered into hers. There was one thing he had been without for months, that he very much wanted to do with her, and only her.

www.ingramcontent.com/pod-product-compliance
Lightning Source LLC
Chambersburg PA
CBHW071541100726
47908CB00004B/1463